HEXTALL Sc.

THREE SHOOTING FROM KING.

DICK TURPIN'S

CELEBRATED

RIDE TO YORK.

CHAPTER I.

THE RENDEZVOUS AT KILBURN.

"Drink deep, my brave boys, of the bastinado,
Of stramazons, tinctures, and slie passatas;
Of the carricado, and rare embrocado,
Of blades, and rapier hilts of surest guard,
Of the Vincentio and Burgundian ward.
Have we not bravely tossed this bombast foil button !
Win gold and wear gold, boys, 'tis we that merit it."
PRINCE OF PRIGS' REVELS.

THE present straggling suburb at the northwest of the metropolis, known as Kilburn, had scarcely been called into existence a century ago, and an ancient hostel, with a few detached farm-houses, were the sole habitations to be found in the present populous vicinage. The place of refreshment for the ruralizing cockney of 1737, was a substantial–looking tenement of the good old stamp, with great bay windows, and a balcony in front, bearing as its ensign, the jovial visage of the lusty knight, Jack Falstaff. Shaded by a spreading elm, a circular bench embraced the aged trunk of the tree; sufficiently tempting, no doubt, to incline the wanderer on those dusty ways to "rest and be thankful," and to cry encore to a frothing tankard of the best ale to be obtained within the chimes of Bow Bells.

Upon a table, as green as the privet and holly that formed the walls of the bower in which it was placed, stood a great china bowl, one of those leviathen memorials of bygone wassailry, which we may sometimes espy (reversed in token of the desuetude) perched on the top of an old japanned closet; but seldom, if ever, encountered in its proper position on its genial board.   All the appliances of festivity were at hand.   Pipes and rummers strewed the board.   Perfume subtle, yet mellow, as of pine and lime, exhaled from out the bowl and mingling with the scent of a neighbouring bed of mignionette, and the subdued odour of the Indian weed, formed altogether as delectable an atmosphere of sweets as one would wish to inhale on a melting August afternoon.   So, at least, thought the inmates of the arbour, nor did they, by any means, confine themselves to the gratification of a single sense.   The ambrosial contents of the china bowl proved as delicious to the taste as its bouquet was grateful to the smell; while the eyesight was soothed by reposing on the smooth sward of a bowling-green, spread out immediately before it, or in dwelling upon gentle undulating meads, terminating, at about a mile's distance, in the woody, spire-crowned heights of Hampstead.

At the left of the table was seated, or rather lounged, a slender, elegant-looking young man, with dark languid eyes, sallow complexion, and features wearing that peculiarly pensive expression, often communicated by dissipation; an expression which, we regret to say, is sometimes found more pleasing than it ought to be in the eyes of the gentle sex.   Habited in a light summer riding dress, fashioned according to the taste of the time, of plain and unpretending material, and rather under than over dressed, he had, perhaps, on that very account, perfectly the air of a gentleman.   There was, altogether, an absence of pretension about him, which, combined with great apparent self-possession, contrasted very forcibly with the vulgar assurance of his showy companions.   The figure of the youth was slight, even to fragility, giving little outward manifestation of the vigour of frame he in reality possessed.   This spark was a no less distinguished personage than Tom King, a noted high-wayman of his time, who obtained, from his appearance and address, the *sobriquet* of the "Gentleman Highwayman."

Tom was indeed a pleasant fellow in his day. His career was brief,

 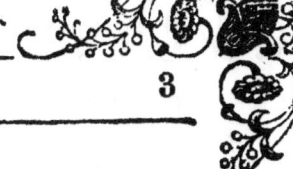

but brilliant: your meteors are ever momentary. He was a younger son of a good family ;—had good blood in his veins—though not a groat in his pockets. According to the old song—

" When he arrived at man's estate,
It was all the estate he had,"

and all the estate he was ever likely to have. Nevertheless, if he had no income, he contrived, as he said, to live as if he had the mines of Peru at his control; a miracle not solely confined to himself. For a moneyless man, he had rather expensive habits. He kept his three nags; and, if fame does not belie him, a like number of mistresses,—nay, if we are to place any faith in certain scandalous chronicles to which we have had access, he was for some time the favoured lover of a celebrated actress, who for the time, supplied him with the means of keeping up his showy establishment, but things could not long hold thus, Tom was a model of infidelity, and that was the only failing his mistress could not overlook, she dismissed him at a moment's notice.

Tom had what Sir Walter Scott happily denominates " an indistinct notion of *meum* and *tuum*," and became confirmed in the opinion, that everything he could lay hands upon constituted lawful spoil, and then, even those he robbed, admitted that he was the most gentleman-like-highwayman they had ever the fortune to meet with, and trusted they might always be so lucky. So popular did he become upon the road that it was accounted a distinction to be stopped by him ; he made a point of robbing none but gentlemen and—Tom's shade would quarrel with us were we to omit them—ladies. His acquaintance with Turpin was singular, and originated in a rencontre. Struck with his appearance, Dick presented a pistol, and bade King deliver. The latter burst into a laugh, and an explanation immediately ensued. Thenceforward they became sworn brothers—the Pylades and Orestes of the road, and though seldom seen together in public, had many a merry moonlight ride in company.

Tom still maintained three mistresses, his valet, his groom (tiger we should have called him), " and many a change of clothes besides,"

says his biographer, "with which he appeared more like a lord then a highwayman?" And what more, we should like to know, would a lord wish to have? Few younger sons, we believe, can boast so much: and it is chiefly on their account, with some remote view to the benefit of the unemployed youth of all professions, that we have enlarged so much upon Tom King's history. The road, we must beg to repeat, is still open ; the chances are greater than they ever were ; we fully believe it is their only road to preferment, and we are sadly in want of highwaymen.

To return to Tom as he was in the arbour. Judging from his manner he appeared to be almost insensible to the presence of his companions, and to be scarcely a partaker in their revelry. His back was towards his immediate neighbour, his glass sparkled untouched at his elbow; and one hand, beautifully white and small, a mark of his birth and breeding (crede Byron), rested upon the edge of the table, while his thin, delicate digits, palpably demonstrative of his faculty of adaptation (crede James Harpy Vaux) were employed with a silver toothpick. In other respects, he seemed to be lost in reverie, and was in all probability meditating new exploits.

The reader, we imagine, will scarcely need to be told who was the owner of those keen, grey eyes; those exuberant red whiskers ; that airy azure frock. it was

> " Our brave co-partner of the roads,
> Skilful surveyors of highways and hedges."

in a word—Dick Turpin!

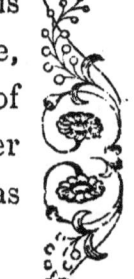

Dick Turpin was a good-humoured, good-looking man, with immense bushy, red whiskers, a freckled, florid complexion, and sandy hair, rather inclined to scantiness towards the scalp of the head, which garnished the nape of his neck with a ruff of crisp curls, like the ring on a monk's shaven crown. Notwithstanding this tendency to baldness, Dick could not be more than thirty, though his looks were some five years in advance. His face was one of those inexpressible countenances which appear to be proper to a peculiar class of men—a regular Newmarket physiognomy—compounded chiefly of cunning and as-

surance; not low cunning, nor vulgar assurance, but crafty sporting subtlety, careless as to results, indifferent to obstacles, ever on the alert for the main chance, game and turf all over, eager, yet easy; keen, yet quiet. He was somewhat showily dressed, in such wise that he looked half like a fine gentleman of that day, half like a jockey of our own. His nether man appeared in well-fitting, well-worn buckskins, and boots with tops, not unconscious of the saddle, while the airy extravagance of his broad-skirted, sky-blue riding coat, the richness of his vest (the pockets of which were beautifully exuberant, according to the mode of 1737), the smart luxuriance of his shirt-frill, and a certain curious taste in the size and style of his buttons, proclaimed that, in his own esteem at least, his person did not appear altogether unworthy of decoration: nor, in justice to Dick, can we allow that he was in error. He was a model of a man for five feet ten; square, compact, capitally built in every particular, excepting that his legs were slightly imbowed, which defect probably arose from his being almost constantly on horseback; a sort of exercise in which he greatly delighted, and was accounted a superb rider.

The companions of Dick Turpin and Tom King were two kindred spirits—a blackleg and a prize-fighter, on whose losing a fight they had a heavy stake. Dick had been called upon to act as president of the board, and an excellent president he made, sedulously devoting himself to the due administration of the punch bowl. Not a rummer was allowed to stand empty for an instant. Toast, sentiment, and anacreontic song, succeeded each other at speedy intervals; but there was no speechifying—no politics. He left Church and State to take care of themselves. Whatever his politics might be, Dick never allowed them to interfere with his pleasures. His maxim was to make the most of the passing moment; the *dum vivimus vivamus* was never out of his mind, a precautionary measure which we recomend to the adoption of all gentlemen of the like, or any other precarious profession.

Notwithstanding all Dick's efforts to promote conviviality, seconded by the excellence of the beverage itself, conversation somehow or other began to flag; from being general it became particular. Tom

King, who was no punch-bibber, especially at that time of day, fell into a deep reverie; your gamesters often do so; the pugilist, who had smoked himself drowsy, was composing himself to a doze; while Turpin passively listened to an harangue from the gambler on his own personal and private affairs.

CHAPTER II.

BLACK BESS.

"Peace, base calumniator!" exclaimed Tom King, aroused from his toothpick reverie by the boisterous and rather severe remarks of the blackleg, in recounting to Turpin the infidelity of his mistress, in which recital he bore rather hardly on the whole petticoated portion of creation, "Peace, I say! None shall dare abuse that dear devoted sex in the hearing of their champion, without my pricking a lance in their behalf. What do you, either of you, who abuse women in that wholesale style, know of her? Nothing—worse then nothing; and yet you venture on your paltry experience, to lift your voices and decry the sex. Now I do know her, and upon my own opinion avouch that as a sex, woman compared with man is as an angel to a devil. As a sex, woman is faithful, loving, and self-sacrificing. We 'tis that make her otherwise, we, selfish, exacting, neglecting men; we teach her indifference, and then blame her apt scholarship. We spoil our own hand, and then blame the cards. No abuse of woman in my hearing. Give me a glass of grog—Dick, the sex—three times three!"

"Well," replied Dick, replenishing King's rummer, "I shan't refuse your toast, though my heart don't respond to your sentiments. Ah, Tom! the sex you praise so much, will, I fear, prove your undoing. Do as you please, but curse me if ever I pin my life to a petticoat."

"Well," said Tom King, "all you can say don't alter my good opinion of the women. No secret have I from the girl of my

TURPIN'S FLIGHT THROUGH EDMONTON.

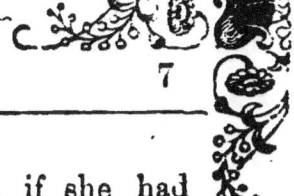

heart. She could have sold me over and over again, if she had chosen. But my sweet Sue is not the wench to do that."

"It is not too late," observed Dick. "Your Dalilah may yet hand you over to the Philistines,"

"Then I shall die in a good cause," said King, " but

> The Tyburn tree
> Has no terrors for me,
> Let better men swing—I'm at liberty.

I shall never come to the scragging post, unless you turn topsman, Dick Turpin. My nativity has been cast, and the stars have declared I am to die by the hand of my best friend—and that's you—eh, Dick ?"

"It sounds like it," replied Turpin; "but I advise you not to become too intimate with Jack Ketch. He may prove your best friend after all."

"Why faith, that's true," replied King, laughing; "and if I must ride backwards up Holborn Hill, I will do the thing in style, and honest Jack Ketch shall never want his dues. A man should always die game. We none of us know how soon our turn may come—but come when it will, I shall never flinch from it.—

> As the highwayman's life is the fullest of zest,
> So the highwayman's death is the briefest and best;
> He dies not as other men die, by degrees,
> But at once ! without flinching—and quite at his ease.

as the song you are so fond of says. When I die it will not be of consumption. And if the surgeon's knife must come near me, it will be after death. There is some comfort in that reflection, at all events."

"True," replied Turpin, " And with a little alteration, my song would suit you capitally ;—

> There is not a king, should you search the world round,
> So blithe as the king's king, Tom King, to be found
> Dear woman's his empire, each girl is his own,
> And he'd have a long reign if he'd let 'em alone,

"Ha, ha !" laughed Tom; "and now, Dick, to change the subject, You are off, I understand, to Yorkshire to-night. Pon my soul, you

are a wonderful fellow—an alibi personified !—here and everywhere at the same time—no wonder you are called the flying highwayman. To day in town, to morrow in York—the day after at Chester.   The devil only knows where you will pitch your quarters a week hence. There are rumours of you in all counties at the same moment.   This man swears you robbed him at Hounslow ; that, on Salisbury Plain ; while another avers you monopolise Cheshire and Yorkshire, and that it is'nt safe even to *hunt* without pops in your pocket.   I heard some devilish good stories of you t'other day—the fellow who told them to me little thought I was a brother blade."

" You flatter me," said Dick, smiling complacently.   " But it's no merit of mine.   Black Bess alone enables me to do it, and her's be the credit. Talking of being everywhere at the same time, you shall hear what she once did for me in Cheshire.   Meantime, a glass to the best mare in England.   You won't refuse that toast, Tom.   Ah ! if your mistress is only as true to you, as my nag to me, you might set at nought the tightest hempen cravat that was ever twisted, and defy your best friend to hurt you.   Black Bess ! and God bless her ! And now for the song." Saying which, with much emotion, Turpin chaunted the following rhymes :—

BLACK BESS.

Let the lover his mistress's beauty rehearse,
And laud her affections in languishing verse ;
Be it mine in rude strains, but with truth to express,
The love that I bear to my bonny Black Bess.

From the West was her dam, from the East was her sire,
From the one came her swiftness, the other her fire,
No peer of the realm better blood can possess,
Than flows in the veins of my bonny Black Bess.

Look ! look ! how that eye-ball glows bright as a brand ;
That neck proudly arches, those nostrils expand ;
Mark—that wide-flowing mane, of which each silky tress
Might adorn prouder beauties though none like Black Bess.

Mark—that skin sleek as velvet, and dusky as night,
With its jet undisfigured by one spot of white ;
That throat branched with veins, prompt to charge or caress,
Now is she not beautiful ?---my bonny Black Bess.

Over highway and byeway, in rough and smooth weather,
Some thousand of miles have we journeyed together,
Our couch the same straw, our meals the same mess,
No couple more constant than I and Black Bess.

By moonlight, in darkness, by night or by day,
My headlong career there is nothing can stay ;
She cares not for distance, she knows not distress.
Can you show me a courser to match with Black Bess.

"Egad, I should think not," exclaimed King; "you are as sentimental on the subject of your mare, as I am when I think of my darling Susan. But pardon my interruption. Pray proceed."

"Let me first clear my throat," returned Dick, " and now to resume :

Once it happened in Cheshire, near Dunham, I popped,
On a horseman alone, whom I speedily stopped ;
That I lightened his pockets, you'll readily guess.
Quick work makes Dick Turpin when mounted on Bess.

Now it seems the man knew me, " Dick Turpin," says he,
" You shall swing for this job, as you live d'ye see ;
I laughed at his threats and vows of redress---
I was sure of an alibi then with Black Bess.

The road was a hollow, a sunken ravine*
Overshadowed completely by wood like a screen,
I clambered the bank, and I needs must confess,
That one touch of the spur grazed the side of Black Bess.

Brake, brook, meadow, and plough'd field, Bess fleetly bestrode,
As the crow wings her flight, we selected our road ;
We arrived at Hough Green in five minutes or less.
My neck it was saved by the speed of Black Bess.

Stepping carelessly forward, I lounge on the green,
Taking excellent care that by all I am seen,
Some remarks on time's flight to the squires I address,
But I say not a word on the flight of Black Bess

I mention the hour—it was just about four—
Play a rubber at bowls—think the danger is o'er ;
When athwart the next game, like a checkmate at chess,
Comes the horseman in search of the rider of Bess.

---

* The exact spot where Turpin committed this robbery, which has often been pointed out to us, lies in what is now a woody hollow, though once the old road from Altringham to Knutsford, skirting the rich and sylvan domains of Dunham, and descending the hill that brings you to the bridge crossing the little river Collin. With some difficulty we penetrated this ravine. It is just the place for an adventure of the kind. A small brook wells through it, and the steep banks are overhung with timber, and were when we last visited the place, in April, 1834, a perfect nest of primroses and wild flowers. Hough (pronounced Hoo) Green, lies about three miles across the country---the way Turpin rode. The old Bowling-green is one of the pleasantest inns in Cheshire.

What matter details ? Off with triumph I came
He swears to the hour, and the squires swear the same,
I had robbed him at four—while at four they profess
I was quietly bowling, all thanks to Black Bess.

Then one halloo ,boys, one loud cheering halloo !
To the swiftest of coursers, the gallant, the true !
For the sportsman unborn shall the memory bless,
Of the horse of the highwayman, bonny Black Bess !

Loud acclamations rewarded Dick's performance.

The party assumed once more a lively air, and the glass was circulated so freely, that at last a final charge drained the ample bowl of its contents.

"The best of friends must part," said Dick, "and I would willingly order another whiff of punch, but I think we have all had *enough to satisfy us*, as you milling coves have it, Zory !—Your one eye has got a drop in it already, old fellow—and, to speak the truth, I must be getting into the saddle without more delay, for I have a long ride before me.   So now, pals, farewell !—a long farewell !" said Dick, in a tone of theatrical valediction, "As I said before, the best friends must separate.   We may soon meet again, or we now may part for ever. We cannot command our luck.   But we can make the best of the span allotted to us.   You have your game to play.   I have mine.   May each of us meet with the success he deserves."

" Egad, I hope not," said King ; " I am afraid in that case the chances would be against us."

" Well, then, the success we anticipate, if you prefer it," rejoined Dick. " I have only to observe one thing more, namely, that I must insist upon standing Sam upon the present occasion.   Not a word, I won't hear a syllable. Landlord, I say—what, ho !" continued Dick, stepping out of the arbour, " Here my old Admiral of the White, what's the reckoning—what's to pay, I say ?"

" Let ye know directly, Sir," replied mine host of the Falstaff.

" Order my horse—the black mare," added Dick.

" And mine," said King, " the sorrel colt.   I will ride with you a mile or two on the road, Dick perhaps we may stumble upon something."

" Very likely."

" We meet at twelve, at D'Osyndar's, Jerry," said King, "if nothing happens."

" Agreed," responded the sharper.

" What say you to a rubber at bowls, in the meantime ?" said the fighting man, taking the pipe from his lips.

Jerry nodded acquiescence. And while they went in search of the instruments of the game, Turpin and King sauntered gently on the green.

It was a delicious evening. The sun was slowly declining, and glowed like a ball of fire amid the thick foliage of a neighbouring elm. Whether, like the robber, Moor, Tom King was touched by this glorious sunset, we pretend not to determine. Certain it was that a shade of inexpressible melancholy passed across his handsome countenance, as he gazed in the direction of Harrow-on-the-Hill, which lying to the west of the green upon which they walked, stood out with its pointed spire and lofty college, against the ruddy sky. He spoke not ; but Dick noticed the passing emotion.

" What ails you, Tom ?" said he with much kindness of manner— " are you not well, lad ?"

" Yes, I am well enough," said King ; " I know not what came over me, but looking at Harrow, I thought of my school-days, and what I was *then*, and that bright prospect reminded me of my boyish hopes."

" Tut—tut," said Dick, " this is idle—you are a man now."

" I know I am," replied Tom ?" but I *have* been a boy. Had I any faith in presentiments, I should say this is the last sunset I shall ever see."

" Here comes our host," said Dick, smiling, "I have no presentiment that this is the last bill I shall ever pay."

The bill was brought and settled. As Turpin paid it, the man's conduct was singular and awakened his suspicious,

" Are our horses ready ?" asked Dick, quickly.

" They are, Sir," said the landlord.

" Let us begone," whispered Dick to King ; " I don't like that fellow's manner. I thought I heard a carriage draw up at the inn door just now—there may be danger. Be fly !" added he to Jerry and the other. " Now, Sir," said he to the landlord, " lead the way. Keep on the alert, Tom."

Dick's hint was not lost upon the two bowlers. They watched their comrades—and listened intently for any manifestation of alarm.

CHAPTER III.

A SURPRISE.

While Turpin and King are walking across the Bowling-green, we will see what has taken place outside the inn. Tom's presentiments of danger were not, it appeared, without foundation. Scarcely had the ostler brought forward our two highwayman's steeds, when a post-chaise, escorted by two or three horsemen, drove furiously up to the door. The sole occupant of the carriage was a lady, whose slight and pretty figure was all that could be distinguished, her face being closely veiled. The landlord, who was busied casting up Turpin's account, rushed forth at the summons. A word or two passed between him and the horseman, upon which the former's countenance fell. He posted in the direction of the garden, and the horsemen instantly dismounted.

" We have him now, sure enough," said one of them, an attorney, named Coates, who, having been stopped by our highwayman, had resolved on capturing him for the public good ; he was accompanied by another sufferer.

" By the powers, I begin to think so," replied the other horseman, " But don't spoil all, Mr. Coates, by being too precipitate."

" Never fear that, Mr. Tyrconnel," said Coates, " he's sure to come for his mare. That's a *trap* certain to catch him, eh, Mr. Paterson.

With the chief constable of Westminster to back us, the devil's in it if we are not a match for him."

"I'd rather you would help *us*, Mr. Paterson;" said Coates; " never mind Tom King, another time will do for him."

" No such thing," said Paterson, " one *weighs* just as much for that matter as t'other. I'll take Tom to myself, and surely you two, with the landlord and ostler, can manage Turpin amongst you."

" I don't know that," said Coates, doubtfully, " he is a devil of a allow to deal with."

" Take him quietly," said Paterson. " Draw the chaise out of the way, lad. Take your tits to one side, and place their nags near the door, ostler. Shall you be able to see him, ma'am, where you are?" asked the chief constable, walking to the carriage, and touching his hat to the lady within. Having received a satisfactory nod from the bonnet and veil, he returned to his companions. " And now, gemmen," added he, " let us step aside a little. " Don't use your fire-arms too soon."

As if conscious of what was passing around her, and of the danger that awaited her master, Black Bess exhibited so much impatience, and plunged so violently, that it was with difficulty the ostler could hold her. " The devil's in the mare," said he; "what is the matter with her? She was quiet enough a few minutes since. So, ho! lass, stand."

Turpin and King, meanwhile walked quickly through the house preceded by the host, who conducted them, not without some inward trepidation, towards the door. Arrived there, each man rushed swiftly to his horse. Dick was in the saddle in an instant, and stamping her foot upon the ostler's leg, Black Bess compelled the man, yelling with pain, to quit his hold of the bridle. Tom King was not equally fortunate. Before he could mount his horse, a loud shout was raised, which startled the animal, and caused him to swerve, so that Tom lost his footing in the stirrup, and fell to the ground. He was instantly seized by Paterson, and a struggle commenced; King endeavouring, but in vain, to draw a pistol.

"Flip him, Dick, fire, or I am taken," cried King. " Fire, d——n you; why don't you fire!" shouted he, in desperation, still struggling vehemently with Paterson, who was a strong man, and more than a match for a light weight like King.

"I can't, cried Dick, " I shall hit you if I fire."

"Take your chance," shouted King, " Is this your friendship."

Thus urged, Turpin fired. The ball ripped up the sleeve of Paterson's coat, but did not wound him.

" Again!" cried King; "shoot him, I say. Don't you hear me? Fire again!"

Pressed as he was by foes on every side, himself their mark, for both Coates and Tyrconnel had fired upon him, and were now mounting their steeds to give chase, it was impossible that Turpin could take sure aim—adding to which, in the struggle, Paterson and King were each moment changing their relative positions. He, however would no longer hesitate, but again fired, at his friend's request. The ball lodged in King's breast! He fell at once. At this instant a shriek was heard from the chaise—the window was thrown open, and her thick veil being drawn aside, the features of a very pretty female, now impressed with terror and contrition, were suddenly exhibited.

King fixed his glazing eyes upon her.

"Susan!" sighed he; "Is it you that I behold."

"Yes, yes, it is she, sure enough," said Paterson, "You see, ma'am, what you and such like have brought him to. However, you will lose your reward—he's going fast enough."

"Reward?" gasped King, "reward! did she betray me?"

"Ay, ay, sir," said Paterson, "she blowed the gaff, if it's any consolation to you to know it."

"Consolation!" repeated the dying man; "perfidious!—oh!—the prophecy—my best friend—Turpin—I die by his hand."

And vainly striving to raise himself, he fell back and expired. Alas! Poor Tom!

"Mr. Paterson! Mr. Paterson!" cried Coates; "leave the landlord to look after the body of that dying ruffian, and mount with us in pursuit of the living rascal. Come, Sir—quick! mount! despatch.—You see he is yonder—he seems to hesitate—we shall have him now."

"Well, gemmen, I am ready," said Paterson; "but how the devil came you to let him escape?"

"Saint Patrick only knows!" said Tyrconnel; "he is as slippery as an eel—and, like a cat, turn him which way you will, he is always sure to alight upon his legs. I would'nt wonder but we lose him now after all, though he has such a small start, That mare flies like the wind."

"He shall have a tight run for it, at all events," said Paterson, putting spurs to his horse. "I've a good nag under me, and you are neither badly mounted. He's only three hundred yards before us, and the devil's in it if we can't run him down. It's a three-hundred pound job, Mr. Coates, and well worth a race.

"You shall have another hundred from me, sir, if you take him," said Coates, urging on his steed.

"Thank you, sir, thank you. Follow my directions, and we'll make sure of him," said the constable. "Gently, gently, not so fast up the hill—you see he's breathing his horse. All in good time, Mr. Coates—all in good time, sir."

And, maintaining an equal distance, both parties cantered leisurely up the ascent now called Windmill Hill. We shall now return to Turpin.

Aghast at the deed he had accidently committed, Dick remained for a few moments irresolute; he perceived that King was mortally wounded, and that all attempts at rescue would be fruitless; he perceived, likewise, that Jerry and the other had effected their escape from the bowling-green, as he could detect their figures stealing along the hedge-side. He hesitated no longer. Turning his horse, he galloped slowly off, little heeding the pursuit in which he was threatened.

"Every bullet has its billet," said Dick; "but little did I think that I should really turn poor Tom's executioner. To the devil with this rascally snapper," cried he, throwing the pistol over the hedge. "I could never have used it again. 'Tis strange, too, that he should have foretold his own fate—devilish strange! And then that he should have been betrayed by the very blowen he trusted! that's a lesson, if I wanted any. But, trust a woman!—not I, the length of my little finger."

CHAPTER IV.

THE HUE AND CRY.

ARRIVED at the brow of the hill, whence such a beautiful view of the country surrounding the metropolis is obtained, Turpin turned for an instant to reconnoitre his pursuers. Coates and Tyrconnel he utterly disregarded, but Paterson was a more formidable foe, and he knew that he had to deal with a man of resolution. It was then, for the first time, that the thoughts of executing his most extraordinary ride to York flashed across him—his bosom throbbed high with rapture, and he involuntarily exclaimed aloud, as he raised himself in the saddle, "By God ! I'll do it !"

He took one last look at the great Babel, that lay buried in a world of trees beneath him—and, as his quick eye ranged over the magnificent prospect, lit up by the gorgeous sunset, he could not help thinking of Tom King's last words. " Poor fellow !" thought Dick, " he said truly. He will never see another sunset." Aroused by the approaching clatter of his pursuers, Dick struck into a lane which leads on the right of the road, now called Shoot-up-hill-lane, and set off at a good pace in the direction of Hampstead.

" Now," cried Paterson, " put your tits to it my boys. We must not lose sight of him for a second in these lanes."

Accordingly, as Turpin was by no means desirous of inconveniencing his mare in this early stage of the business, and as the ground was still upon an ascent, the parties observed their relative distances.

At length, after various twistings and turnings in that deep and devious lane : after scaring one or two farmers, and riding over a brood or two of ducks ; dipping into the verdant valley of West End, and ascending another hill, Turpin burst upon the gorsey, sandy, and beautiful heath of Hampstead. Shaping his course to the left, Dick then made for the lower part of the heath, and skirted a path that leads

towards North End, passing the furze-crowned summit, which is now crested by a clump of lofty pines.

It was here that the chase first assumed a character of interest. Being open ground, the pursued and pursuers were in full view of each other, and, as Dick rode swiftly across the heath, with the shouting trio hard at his heels, the scene had a very animated appearance. He crossed the hill—the Hendon-road—passed Crackskull-common, and dashed along the cross-road to Highgate.

Hitherto, no advantage had been gained by the pursuers; they had not lost ground, but still they had not gained an inch, and much spurring was required to maintain their position. As they approached Highgate, Dick slackened his pace, and the other party redoubled their efforts. To avoid the town, Dick struck into a narrow path at the right, and rode easily down the hill.

His pursuers were now within a hundred yards, and shouted to him to stand. Pointing to a gate which seemed to bar their further progress, Dick unhesitatingly charged it, clearing it in a beautiful style. Not so with Coates's party. And the time they had lost in unfastening the gate, which none of them chose to leap, enabled Dick to put additional space betwixt them. It did not, however, appear to be his intention altogether to outstrip his pursuers; the chase seemed to give him excitement, which he was willing to prolong, as much as was consistent with his safety. Scudding rapidly past Highgate, like a swift sailing schooner, with three lumbering Indiamen in her wake, Dick now took the lead along a narrow lane that threads the fields, in the direction of Hornsey. The shouts of his followers had brought others to join them, and as he neared Crouch End, traversing the lane which takes its name from Du Val, and in which a house frequented by that gayest of robbers, stands, or stood, "A highwayman! A highwayman!" rang in his ears, in a discordant chorus of many voices.

The whole neighbourhood was alarmed by the cries, and by the tramp of horses—the men of Hornsey rushed into the road to see the fugitive—the women held up their babes to catch a glimpse of the

flying cavalcade, which seemed to gain numbers and animation as it advanced. Suddenly three horsemen appear in the road, they hear the uproar and din. "A highwayman! A highwayman!" cry the voices; "stop him, stop him!" But it is no such easy matter. With a pistol in each hand, and his bridle in his teeth, Turpin passed boldly on. His fierce looks—his furious steed—the impetus with which he pressed forward, bore down all before him. The horsemen gave way, and only served to swell the list of his pursuers.

"We have him now—we have him now!" cried Paterson, exultingly. "Shout for your lives—the Turnpike man will hear us—shout again!—again! The fellow has heard it. The gate is shut. We have him—ha! ha!"

The old Hornsey toll-bar was a high gate, with *cheveux de frize* on the upper rail—it may be so still. The gate was swung into its lock, and, like a tiger in his lair, the prompt custodian of the turnpike trust, ensconced within his doorway, held himself in readiness to spring upon the runaway. But Dick kept steadily on. He coolly calculated the height of the gate; he looked to the right and to the left, nothing better offered; he spoke a few words of encouragement to Bess, gently patted her neck, then struck spurs into her sides, and cleared the spikes by an inch. Out rushed the amazed turnpike man, thus unmercifully bilked, and was nearly trampled to death under the feet of Paterson's horse.

"Open the gate, fellow, and be expeditious," shouted the chief constable.

"Not I!" said the man sturdily, "unless I get my dues. I've been done once already. But strike me stupid if I am done a second time."

"Don't you perceive that's a highwayman? don't you know that I'm chief constable of Westminster?" said Paterson, showing his staff. "How dare you oppose me in the discharge of my duty?"

"That may be, or may not be," said the man, doggedly. "But you don't pass, unless I get the blunt, and that's the long and short on it."

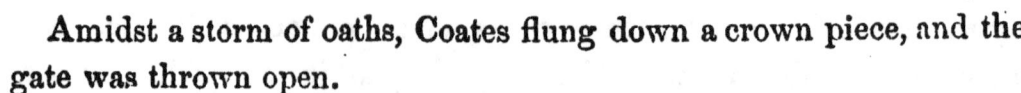

Amidst a storm of oaths, Coates flung down a crown piece, and the gate was thrown open.

Turpin took advantage of this delay to breathe his mare ; and striking into a bye-lane, at Duckett's Green, cantered easily along in the direction of Tottenham. Little repose was allowed him ; yelling like a pack of hounds in full cry, his pursuers were again at his heels. He had now to run the gauntlet of the long straggling town of Tottenham, and various were the devices of the populace to entrap him. The whole place was up in arms, shouting, screaming, running, dancing, and hurling every possible description of missile at the horse and her rider. Dick merrily rosponded to their clamour, as he flew past, and laughed at the brick-bats that were showered, thick as hail, and quite as harmlessly, around him.

A few more miles hard riding tired the volunteers, and before the chase reached Edmonton, most of them were "*no where.*" Here fresh relays were gathered, and a strong field was again mustered. John Gilpin, himself, could not have excited more astonishment amongst the good folks of Edmonton, then did our highwayman, as he galloped through their town. Unlike the man of Tottenham, the mob received him with acclamations, thinking no doubt, that, like " the citizen of famous London town," he rode for a wager. Presently, however, borne on the wings of the blast, came the cries of " Turpin ! Dick Turpin !" and the hurrahs were changed to hootings—but such was the rate at which our highwayman rode, that no serious opposition could be offered to him.

A man in a donkey cart, unable to get out of the way, drew himself up in the middle of the road. Turpin treated him as he had done the *dub* at the *knaping jigger*, and cleared the driver and his little wain with ease. This was a capital stroke, and well adapted to please the multitude, who are ever taken with a brilliant action. "Hark away, Dick !" resounded on all hands—while hisses were as liberally bestowed upon his pursuers.

THE PHANTOM.

CHAPTER V.

THE SHORT PIPE.

AWAY they fly, past scattered cottages, swiftly and skimmingly, like eagles on the wing, along the Enfield Highway. All were well mounted, and their horses, now thoroughly warmed, had got into their paces, and did their work beautiful. None of Coates's party lost ground, but they maintained it at the expense of their steeds, which were streaming like water-carts, while Black Bess had not turned a hair.

Turpin, the reader already knows, was a crack rider; he was the crack rider of England of his time, and, perhaps of any time. The craft and mystery of jockeyship was not then so well understood as it is in the nineteenth century, men treated their horses differently, and few rode them as well as most ride now, when every youngster takes to the field as naturally as if he had been bred a Guacho. Dick Turpin was a glorious exception to the rule, and anticipated a later age. He rode wonderfully light, yet sat his saddle to perfection, distributing the weight so exquisitely, that his horse scarcely felt his pressure; he yielded to every movement made by the animal, and became, as it were, part and parcel of itself—he took care Bess should be neither strained nor wrung. Freely, and as lightly as a feather, was she borne along; beautiful was it to see her action; to watch her style and temper of covering the ground; and many a first-rate Meltonian might have got a wrinkle from Turpin's seat and conduct.

We have before stated that it was not Dick's object to ride away from his pursuers; he could have done that at any moment; he liked the fun of the chase, and would have been sorry to put a period to his own excitement. Confident in his mare, he just kept her at such speed as should put his pursuers completely to it, without, in the

slightest degree inconveniencing himself. Some judgment of the speed at which they went may be formed, when we state that little better than an hour had elapsed, and nearly twenty miles had been ridden over. "Not bad travelling that" methinks we hear the reader exclaim.

"By the mother that bore me," said Tyrconnel, as they went along in this slapping style—he, by-the-by, rode a big, Roman-nosed, powerful horse, well adapted for his weight, but which required a plentiful exercise both of leg and arm, to call forth all his action, and keep the rider alongside his companions. "By the mother that bore me," said he, almost thumping the wind out of his flea-bitten Bucephalus with his calves, after the Irish fashion, "if the fellow is'nt lighting his pipe! I saw the sparks fly on each side of him, and there he goes, like a smoky chimney on a frosty morning! See, he turns his impudent phiz, with the pipe in his mouth! are we to stand that, Mr. Coates?"

"Wait awhile, sir; wait awhile," said Coates, "we'll smoke him by-and-by.

Pæens have been sung in honour of the Peons of the Pampas by the *Head*long Sir Francis—but what the gallant major extols so loudly in the South American horsemen, viz, the lighting of a cigar when in full career, was accomplished with equal ease by our English highwayman, a hundred years ago, nor was it esteemed by him an extravagant feat either. Flint, steel, and tinder, were stowed within Dick's ample pouch, the short pipe was at hand, and within a few seconds their was a stream of vapour exhaling from his lips, like the smoke from a steamboat shooting down the river, and tracking its still rapid course through the air.

"I'll let 'em see what I think of 'em," said Dick, coolly, as he turned his head.

It was grey twilight. The mists of coming light were weaving a thin curtain over the rich surrounding landscape. All the sounds and hum of that delicious hour were heard, broken only by the regular clatter of the horses' hoofs. Tired of shouting, the chasers now kept on their way in deep silence—each man held his breath, and plunged

his spurs, rowel deep, into his horse, but the animals were already at the top of their speed, and incapable of greater exertion. Paterson, who, was a hard rider, and perhaps a trifle better mounted, kept the lead—the rest followed as they might.

Had it been undisturbed by the rush of the calvalcade, the scene would have been still and soothing. Overhead a cloud of rooks were winging their garrulous flight to the ancestral avenue of an ancient mansion to the right—the bat was on the wing—the distant lowing of a herd of kine saluted the ear at intervals—the blithe whistle of the rustic herdsman, and the merry chime of waggon bells rang pleasantly from afar. But these cheering sounds, which make the still twilight hour delightful, were lost in the tramp of the horsemen, now three abreast. The hind fled to the hedge for shelter—and the waggoner pricked up his ears, and fancied he heard the distant rumbling of an earthquake.

On rushed the pack, whipping, spurring, tugging for very life. Again they gave voice, in hopes the waggoner might succeed in stopping the fugitive. But Dick was already by his side. "Harkee my tulip," cried he, taking the pipe from his mouth as he passed, "tell my friends behind, they will hear of me at York."

"What did he say?" asked Paterson, coming up the next moment.

"That you'll find him at York," replied the waggoner.

"At York!" echoed Coates, with amazement.

Turpin was now out of sight, and although our trio flogged with all their might and main, they could never catch a glimpse of him, until, within a short distance of Ware, they beheld him at the door of a little public house, standing with his bridle in his hand, coolly quaffing a tankard of ale. No sooner were they in sight, than Dick vaulted into the saddle and rode off.

"Devil seize you, sir! Why did'nt you stop him?" exclaimed Paterson, as he rode up. "My horse is dead lame, I cannot go any further. Do you know what a prize you have missed? Do you know who that was?"

"No, sir, I don't," said the publican. "But I know he gave his mare more ale than he took himself, and he has given me a guinea instead of a shilling. He's a regular good 'un."

"A good 'un!" said Paterson; "it was Turpin, the notorious highwayman. We are in pursuit of him. Have you any horses? our cattle are all blown."

"You'll find the post-house in the town, gentlemen. I'm sorry I can't accommodate you. But I keeps no stabling. I wish you a very good evening, sir," saying which, the publican retreated to his domicile.

"That's a flash crib, I'll be bound," said Paterson. "I'll chalk you down, my friend, you may rely upon it. Thus far we are done, Mr. Coates. But curse me if I give it in. I'll follow him to the world's end first."

"Right, sir—right," said the attorney. "A very proper spirit, Mr. Constable. You will be guilty of neglecting your duty, were you to act otherwise. You must recollect my father, Mr. Paterson Christopher, or Kit Coates. A name as well known at the Old Bailey as Jonathan Wild's. You recollect him—eh?"

"Perfectly well, sir," replied the chief constable.

"The greatest thief-taker, though I say it," continued Coates, "on record. I inherit all his zeal—all his ardour. Come along, sir. We shall have a fine moon in an hour—bright as day—to the post-house! to the post-house!"

Accordingly, to the post-house they went. And, with as little delay as circumstances admitted, fresh hacks being procured, accompanied by a postilion, the party again pursued their onward course, encouraged to believe they were still in the right scent.

Night had now spread her mantle over the earth; still it was not wholly dark. A few stars were twinkling in the deep, cloudless heaven, and a pearly radiance in the eastern horizon, heralded the rising of the orb of night. A gentle breeze was stirring—the dews of evening had already fallen; and the air bland and dry. It was just that beautifully calm night one would have chosen for a ride, if he ever rode by choice at such an hour; and to Turpin, whose chief

excursions were conducted by night, it appeared little less than heavenly.

Full of ardour and excitement, determined to execute what he had mentally undertaken, Turpin held on his solitary course. Everything was favourable to his project; the roads were in admirable condition, his mare was in light order; she was inured to hard work, had rested sufficiently in town to recover from the fatigue of her recent journey, and had never been in more perfect training. "She has now got her wind in her," said Dick, "I'll see what she can do—hark away, lass—hark away! I wish they could see her now," added he, as he felt her almost fly with him.

Encouraged by her master's voice and hand, Black Bess started forward at a pace which few horses could have equalled, and scarcely any have sustained so long. Even Dick, accustomed as he was to her magnificent action, felt electrified at the speed with which he was borne along. "Bravo! Bravo! shouted he—hark away, Bess!"

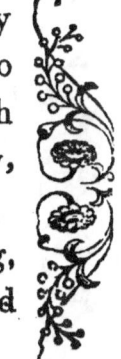

The deep and solemn woods, through which they were rushing, rang with his shouts and the rattle of Bess's hoofs; and thus he held his way, while, in the words of the ballad :—

> " Fled past, on right and left, how **fast**,
> Each forest, grove and bower;
> On right, and left, fled past, how **fast**,
> Each city, town, and tower."

CHAPTER VI.

AGAIN BLACK BESS.

BLACK BESS being, undoubtedly, the heroine of our tale, we may, perhaps, be pardoned for expatiating a little in this place, upon her birth, parentage, breeding, appearance, and attractions. And first as to her pedigree—for, in the horse, unlike the human species, nature has strongly impressed the noble or ignoble caste. He is the real aristrocrat, and the pure blood that flows in the veins of the gallant steed will infallibly be transmitted, if his mate be suitable, throughout all his line. Bess was no *cock tail*. She was thorough bred—she boasted blood in every bright and branching vein:—

> "If blood can give nobility,
>   A noble steed was she ;
> Her sire was blood, and blood her dam,
>   Aud all her pedigree.'

As to her pedigree. Her sire was a desert Arab, renowned in his day, and brought to this country by a wealthy traveller—her dam was an English racer, coal black as her child. Bess united all the fire and gentleness, all the strength and hardihood, the abstinence and endurance of fatigue, of the one—with the spirit and extraordinary fleetness of the other. How Turpin became possessed of her is of little consequence. We never heard that he paid a heavy price for her; though we doubt if any sum would have induced him to part with her. In colour, she was perfectly black, with a skin smooth on the surface as polished jet—not a single white hair cou'd be detected in her satin coat. In make, she was magnificent. Every point was perfect, beautiful, compact; modelled, in little, for strength and speed. Arched was her neck, as that of the swan; clean and fine were her lower limbs, as those of the gazelle; round, and sound as a drum, was her carcass, and as broad as a cloth-yard shaft her width of chest. Hers were the "*pulchre clunes breve caput, arduaque cervix.*" of the Roman bard. There was no redundancy of flesh, it is true, her flanks might, to please some tastes, have been rounder and her shoulder fuller, but look at the nerve and sinew, palpable through the veined limbs! She was built more for strength than beauty, and yet she was beautiful. Look at that elegant little head; those thin taper-ing ears, closely placed together; that broad snorting nostril which seems to snuff the gale with disdain; that eye, glowing and large as the diamond of Giamschid! Is she not beautiful? How splendid her paces! How gracefully she moves! She is off!—no eagle on the wing could skim the air more swiftly. Is she not superb? As to her temper, the lamb is not more gentle—a child might guide her.

But hark back to Dick Turpin. We left him rattling along in superb style, and in the highest possible glee. He could not, in fact, be otherwise than exhilarated, nothing being so wildly intoxicating as a mad gallop. We seem to start out of ourselves — to be endued, for the time, with new energies. Our thoughts take wings rapid as our steed. We feel as if his fleetness and boundless impulses were for the moment our own. We laugh, we exult, we shout for very joy. We cry out with Mephistopheles, but in any thing but a sardonic mood, "What I enjoy with spirit, is it less my own on that account? If I

No. 5.

can pay for six horses, are not their powers mine? I drive along, and am a proper man, as if I had four-and-twenty legs." These were Turpin's sentiments precisely.   Give him four legs and a wide plain, and he needed no Mephistopheles to bid him ride to perdition, as fast as his nag could carry him. Away! away!—the road is level, the path is clear. Press on, thou gallant steed, no obstacle is in thy way—and lo!—the moon breaks forth! Her silvery light is thrown over the woody landscape. Dark shadows are cast athwart the road; and the flying figures of thy rider and thyself are traced, like giant phantoms, in the dust!

Away! away! our breath is gone in keeping up with this tremendous run. Yet Dick Turpin has not lost his wind, for we hear his cheering cry. Hark! he sings. The reader will bear in mind that Oliver means the moon; to "whiddle" is to blab.

OLIVER WHIDDLES.

Oliver whiddles—the tattler old!
Telling what best had been left untold.
Oliver ne'er was a friend of mine;
All glims I hate that so brightly shine.
Give me a night black as hell, and then
See what I'll show to you, my merry men.

Oliver whiddles!—who cares—who cares,
If down upon us he peers and stares?
Mind him who will, with his great white face,
Boldly I'll ride by his glim to the chase;
Give him a Rowland, and loudly as ever
Shout, as I show myself, "Stand and deliver!"

"Egad," soliloquised Dick, looking up at the moon. "old Noll's no bad fellow either. I wouldn't be without his white face to-night for a trifle. He's as good as a lamp to guide one, and let Bess only hold on as she goes now, and I'll do it with ease. Softly wench, softly—dost not see it's a hill we're rising? The devil's in the mare, she cares for nothing." And, as they ascended the hill, Dick's voice once more awoke the echoes of night, by chanting the following reminiscence of his interview with one of his old chums, on Bagshot Heath.

WILL DAVIES AND DICK TURPIN.

One night, when mounted on my mare,
To Bagshot-heath I did repair,
And saw Will Davies hanging there.
Upon the gibbet bleak and bare,
  With a rustified, fustified, mustified air!

Within his chains Wild Will looked blue,
Gone were his sword and snappers too,
Which served their master well and true ;
Says I, " Will Davies, how are you ?
  With your rustified, fustified, mustified air !"

Says he, " Dick Turpin, here I be,
Upon the gibbet as you see :
I take the matter easily,
You'll have your turn as well as me :
  With your whistle-me, pistol-me, cut-my-throat air !"

Says I, " That's very true, my lad ;
Meantime, with pistol and with prad,
I'm quite contented as I am,
And heed the gibbet not a d—n!
  With its rustified, fustified, mustified air !"

"Poor Will Davies !" sighed Dick : " Bagshot ought never to forget him." (1).

For never more shall Bagshot see
A highwayman of such degree,
Appearance, and gentility,
As Will, who hangs upon the tree,
  With his rustified, fustified, mustified air!

"Well," mused Turpin, "I suppose one day it will be with me like all the rest of 'em, and that I shall dance a long lavolta to the music of the four whistling winds, as my betters have done before me ; but I trust whenever the chaunter culls and last speech scribblers get hold of me, they'll at least put no cursed nonsense into my mouth,

---

(1). This, I regret to say, is not the case. The memory of Wild Will Davies, the "Golden Farmer" (so named from the circumstance of his always paying his rent in gold), is fast declining upon his peculiar domain, Bagshot. The inn, which once bore his name, still remains to point out to the traveller the dangers his forefathers had to encounter in crossing this extensive heath. Just beyond the house the common spreads out for miles on all sides in a most gallop-inviting style ; and the passenger, as he gazes from the box of some flying coach, as I have done, upon the gorse-covered waste, may, without much stretch of fancy, imagine he beholds Will Davies careering, like the wind, over its wild and undulating expanse. I am sorry to add, that the "Golden Farmer" has altered its designation to the "Jolly Farmer." This should be amended ; and when next I pass that way, I hope to see the original sign restored. We cannot afford to lose our golden farmers.

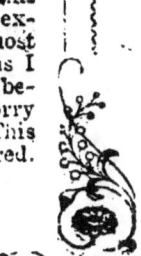

but make me speak.; as I have ever felt, like a man who never either feared death or turned his back upon his friend. In the meantime I'll give them something to talk about. This ride of mine shall ring in their ears long after I'm done for—put to bed with a mattock, and tucked up with a spade."

And when I'm gone, boys, each huntsman shall say,
None rode like Dick Turpin, so far in a day !

" And thou, too, brave Bess !—thy name shall be linked with mine and we'll go down to posterity together ; and what," added he, despondingly, " if it should be too much for thee ? what if—but no matter ! Better die now, while I am with thee, than fall into the knacker's hands. Better die with all thy honours upon thy head, than drag out thy old age at the sand cart. Hark forward, lass— hark forward ! "

By what peculiar instinct is it that this noble animal, the horse, will at once perceive the slightest change in his rider's physical temper- ament, and allow himself so to be influenced by it, that, according as his master's spirits fluctuate, will his own energies rise and fall, wavering

From walk to trot, from canter to full speed ?

How is it, we ask of those more intimately acquainted with the me- taphysics of the huoyhnymn than we pretend to be? Do the saddle or the rein convey, like metallic tractons, vibrations of the spirit be- twixt the two ? We know not—but this much is certain, that no servant partakes so much of the character of his master as the horse. The steed we are wont to ride becomes a portion of ourselves. He thinks and feels with us. As we are lively, he is sprightly ; as we are depressed, his courage droops. In proof of this, let the reader see what horses some men make—*make* we say, because, in such hands

their character is wholly altered. Partaking in a measure of the courage and firmness of the hand that guides them—what their rider wills they do, or strive to do. When that governing power is relaxed their energies are relaxed likewise; and their fine sensibilities supply them with an instant knowledge of the disposition and capacity of the rider. A gift of the gods is the gallant steed, which, like any other faculty we possess, to use and abuse—to command or to neglect—rests with ourselves; he is the best general test of our own self-government.

Black Bess's action amply verified what we have just asserted; for during Turpin's momentary despondency, her pace was perceptibly diminished, and her force retarded—but as he revived she rallied instantly, and, seized apparently with a kindred enthusiasm, snorted joyously as she recovered her speed. Now was it that the child of the desert showed herself the undoubted offspring of the hardy loins from whence she sprung. Full fifty miles had she sped, yet she showed no symptoms of distress. If possible, she appeared fresher than when she started. She had breathed, her limbs were suppler; her action was free; easier, lighter. Her sire, who upon his trackless wilds could have outstripped the pestilent simoon; and with throat unslaked and hunger unappeased, could thrice have seen the scorching sun go down, had not greater powers of endurance. His vigour was her heritage. Her dam, who upon the velvet sod was of almost unapproachable swiftness, and who had often brought her owner golden assurances of her worth, could scarce have kept pace with her, and would have sunk under a third of her fatigue. But Bess was a paragon. We ne'er shall look upon her like again, unless we can prevail upon some Bedouin chief to present us with a brood mare, and then the racing world shall see what a breed we will introduce into this country. Eclipse, Childers, or Hambletonian, shall be nothing to our colt, and even the rail-road slow travelling compared with the speed of our new nags.

But to return to Bess, or rather to go along with her, for there is no halting now; we are going at the rate of twenty knots an hour—

sailing before the wind; and the reader must either keep pace with us, or drop astern. Bess is now in her speed, and Dick happy. Happy!—he is enraptured—maddened—furious—intoxicated as with wine. Pshaw! wine could never throw him into such a burning delirium. Its choicest juices have no inspiration like this. Its fumes are slow and heady. This is ethereal, transporting. His blood spins through his veins, winds round his heart, mounts to his brain. Away! away! He is wild with joy. Hall, cot, tree, tower, glade, mead, waste, or woodland, are seen, passed, left behind, and vanish as in a dream Motion is scarcely perceptible—it is impetus! volition! The horse and her rider are driven forward as it were by self-accelerated speed. A hamlet is visible in the moonlight. It is scarcely discovered, ere the flints sparkle beneath the mare's hoofs. A moment's clatter upon the stones, and it is left behind. Again, it is the silent smiling country. Now they are buried in the darkness of woods; now sweeping along the wide plain; now clearing the unopened toll-bar; now trampling over the hollow-sounding bridge, their shadows momentarily reflected in the placid mirror of the stream; now scaling the hill side a thought more slowly—now plunging, as the horses of Phœbus into the ocean, down its precipitous sides.

The limits of two shires are already past. They are within the confines of a third. They have entered the merry county of Huntingdon—they have surmounted the gentle hill that slips into Godmanchester. They are by the banks of the rapid Ouse. The bridge is passed, and as Turpin rode through the deserted streets of Huntingdon, he heard the eleventh hour given from the iron tongue of St. Mary's spire. In four hours (it was about seven when he started) Dick had accomplished full sixty miles.

A few reeling topers in the streets saw the horseman flit past, and one or two windows were thrown open; but peeping Tom of Coventry would have had small chance of beholding the unveiled beauties of Lady Godiva, had she ridden at the rate of Dick Turpin. He was gone like a meteor, almost as soon as he appeared.

Huntingdon is left behind, and he is once more surrounded by

dew-gemmed hedges, and silent slumbering trees. Broad meadows, or pasture land, with drowsy cattle, or low bleating sheep, lie on either side. But what, to Turpin, at that moment, is nature, animate or inanimate? He thinks only of his mare—his future fame. None are by to see him ride—no stimulating plaudits ring in his ears—no thousand hands are clapping—no thousand voices are huzzaing—no handkerchiefs are waving—no necks strained—no bright eyes rain influence upon him—no eagle orbs watch his motion—no bells are rung—no cup awaits his achievement—no sweepstakes—no plate. But his will be renown—everlasting renown : his will be fame which will not die with him ; which will keep his reputation, albeit a tarnished one, still in the mouths of men. He wants all these adventitious excitements, but he has that within which is a greater excitement that all these. He is conscious that he is doing a deed to live by. If not riding for *life*, he is riding for *immortality*, and as the hero may perchance feel (for even an highwayman may feel like an hero), when he willingly throws away his existence in the hope of earning a glorious name, Turpin cared not what might befall him, so as he could proudly signalize himself as the first in the land,

> To witch the world with noble horsemanship.

What need had he of spectators? *The eye of posterity* was upon him; he felt the influence of that Argus glance, which has made many a poor wight spur on his Pegasus with not half so good a chance of reaching the goal as Dick Turpin. Multitudes, yet unborn, he knew would hear, and laud his deeds. He trembled with excitement, and Bess trembled under him. But the emotion was transient—on, on they fly! The torrent leaping from the craig—the bolt from the bow—the air cleaving eagle—thoughts themselves, are scarce more winged in their flight!"

CHAPTER VII.

THE YORK STAGE.

THE night had hitherto been balmy and beautiful, with a bright array of stars, and a golden harvest moon, which seemed to diffuse even warmth with its radiance; but now Turpin was approaching the region of fog and fen, and he began to feel the influence of that dark atmosphere. The intersecting dykes, yarners, gullies—or whatever they are called—began to send forth their streaming vapours, and chilled the soft and wholesome air, obscuring the void, and in some instances as it were, choking up the road itself with vapours. But fog or fen was the same to Bess, her hoofs rattled merrily along the road, and she burst from a cloud, like Æous at the break of dawn.

It chanced, as he issued from a fog of this kind, that Turpin burst upon the York Stage Coach. It was no uncommon thing for the coach to be stopped; and so furious was the career of our highwayman, that the man involuntarily drew up his horses. Turpin had also to draw in his rein, a task of no little difficulty, as charging a huge lumbering coach, with its full complement of passengers, was more even than Bess could accomplish. The moon shone brightly on Turpin and his mare. He was unmasked, and his features were distinctly visible. An exclamation was uttered by a gentleman on the box, who it appeared instantly recognised him.

"Pull up—draw your horses across the road," cried the gentleman. "That's Dick Turpin, the highwayman. His capture would be worth three hundred pounds to you," added he, addressing the coachman, "and is of equal importance to me. Stand!" shouted he, presenting a cocked pistol.

The resolution of the gentleman was not apparently agreeable

THE GIBBET.

either to the coachman or the majority of the passengers—the name of Turpin acting like magic upon them. One man jumped off behind and was with difficulty afterwards recovered, having tumbled into a deep ditch at the road side. An old gentleman with a cotton night-cap, who had popped out his head to swear at the coachman, drew it suddenly back. A faint scream in a female key issued from within, and there was a considerable hubbub on the roof. Amongst other ominous sounds, the guard was heard to click his long horse-pistols.

"Stop the York four-day stage!" said he, forcing his smoky voice through a world of throat-embracing shawl; "the fastest coach in the kingdom: vos ever sich atrocity heard of? I say Joe, keep them ere leaders steady—we shall all be in the ditch. Don't you see where the hind wheels are? Who—whoop, I say,"

The gentleman on the box now discharged his pistol, and the confusion within was redoubled. The white nightcap was popped out like a rabbit's head, and as quickly popped back, on hearing the highwayman's voice. Owing to the plunging of the horses, the gentleman missed his aim.

Prepared for such emergencies as the present, and seldom at any time taken aback, Dick received the fire without flinching. He then lashed the horses out of his course, and rode up, pistol in hand, to the gentleman, who had fired, "Major Mowbray," said he, in a stern voice, "I know you, we have met before, I meant not either to assault you, or these gentlemen. Yet, you have attempted my life, sir, a second time. But you are now in my power, and, by hell! if you do not answer my demands, nothing earthly shall save you."

Turpin's tone was too imperative to be slighted, and he speedily received the purses of the terrified passengers, the last complier being the officer on the box-seat.

"A thousand thanks, major. Good night to you gentleman," said Dick, laughing.

"Take that with you, and remember the guard," cried the fellow, who, unable to take aim from where he sat, had crept along the coach roof, and discharged thence one of his large horse-pistols at what he

took to be the highwayman's head, but which, luckily for Dick, was his hat, which he had raised to salute the passengers.

"Remember you," said Dick, coolly replacing his perforated beaver on his brow, "you may rely upon it my fine fellow, I'll not forget you the next time we meet."

And off he went, like the breath of a whirlwind.

CHAPTER VIII.

A ROAD-SIDE INN.

WE will now make inquiries after Mr. Coates and his party, of whom we and Dick Turpin have for some time lost sight. With unabated ardour, the vindictive man of law and myrmidons pressed forward. A tacit compact seemed to have been entered into between the highwayman and his pursuers, that he was to fly while they were to follow. Like bloodhounds, they kept steadily upon his trail; nor were they so far behind as Dick imagined. At each post-house they passed, they obtained fresh horses, and, while these were saddling, a post-boy was despatched, *en courier*, to order fresh relays at the next station. In this manner they proceeded after the first stoppage without interruption. Horses were in waiting for them, as they, "bloody with spurring, fiery hot with haste," and their jaded hacks arrived. Turpin had been heard or seen of in all quarters. Turnpike men, waggoners, carters, trampers, all had seen him. Beside, strange as it may seem, they placed some faith in his word. York, they believed, would be his destination.

At length the coach which Dick had encountered hove in sight.

There was another stoppage and another hubbub. The old gentleman's nightcap was again manifested, and suffered a sudden occultation, as upon the former occasion. The post-boy who was in advance, had halted, and given up his horse to Major Mowbray, who exchanged his seat on the box for the saddle, determining, after his interview with Turpin, to return rather than to proceed to town. The post-boy was then placed behind Coates, as being the lightest weight—and, thus reinforced, the party pushed forward as rapid as heretofore.

Eighty and odd miles had now been traversed—the boundary of another county, Northampton, had been passed—yet, no rest, no respite, had Dick Turpin, or his unflinching mare, enjoyed. But here he deemed it fitting to make a brief halt, in order to recruit their somewhat relaxing energies.

Bordering the beautiful domains of Burleigh House, stood a little retired hostelrie, of some antiquity, which bore the great Lord Treasurer's arms. With this house Dick was not altogether unacquainted. The lad who acted as ostler was known to him. It was now midnight, but a bright and beaming night. To the door of the stable then did he ride, and knocked in a peculiar manner. Reconnoitering Dick through a broken pane of glass in the lintel, and apparently satisfied with his scrutiny, the lad thrust forth a head of hair as full of straw as Mad Tom's is represented to be upon the stage. A chuckle of welcome followed his sleepy salutation.

"Glad to see you Captain Turpin," said he; "can I do anything for you?"

"Get me a couple of bottles of brandy, and a beef-steak," said Dick.

"As to the brandy, you can have that in a jiffy—but the steak, Lord love ye, the old 'oman won't stand it at this time; but there's a cold round, mayhap a slice of that might do—or a knuckle of ham."

"D—n your knuckles, Ralph," cried Dick, "have you any raw meat in the house?"

"Raw meat!" echoed Ralph, in surprise; "oh, yes, there's a rare rump ef beef. You can have a cut off that if you like.

"That's the thing I want," said Dick, ungirthing his mare; "give me the scraper—there—I can get a whisp of straw from your head. Now run and get the brandy—better bring three bottles—uncork 'em, and let me have half a pail of water to mix with the spirit."

"A pail-full of brandy and water to wash down a raw steak—my eyes!" exclaimed Ralph, opening wide his sleepy peepers, adding, as he went about the execution of his task, "I always thought them rum-padders, as they call themselves, rum fellows, but now I am sartin on it."

The most sedulous groom could not have bestowed more attention upon the horse of his heart, than Dick Turpin now paid to his mare. He scraped, chafed, and dried her, sounded each muscle, traced each sinew, pulled her ears, examined the state of her feet, and, ascertaining that her "withers were unwrung," finally washed her from head to feet in the diluted spirit; not, however, before he had conveyed a portion of the liquid to his own parched throat, and replenished what Falstaff called a "pocket-pistol," which he had about him. While Ralph was engaged rubbing her down after her bath, Dick occupied himself, not in dressing the raw steak in the manner the stable-boy had anticipated, but in rolling it round the bit of his bridle.

"She'll go now as long as there's breath in her body," said he, putting the flesh-covered iron in her mouth.

The saddle being once more replaced, after champing a moment or two at the bit, Bess began to snort and paw the earth, as if impatient of delay—and, acquainted as he was with her indomitable spirit and power, her condition was a surprise to Dick himself. Her vigour seemed inexhaustible, her vivacity was not a whit diminished, but as she was led into the open space, her step became as light and free as when she started on her ride, and her sense of sound as quick as ever. Suddenly she pricked her ears, and uttered a low neigh. A dull tramp was audible.

"Ha!" exclaimed Dick, springing into the saddle, "they come."

" Who come, captain ?" asked Ralph.

" The road takes a turn here—don't it ?" asked Dick, " sweeps round to the right by the plantations in the hollow ?"

" Ay, ay, captain," answered Ralph, " it's plain you knows the ground."

" What lies behind yon shed ?"

" A stiff fence, captain—a reg'lar rasper—beyond that a hill-side, steep as a house—no oss as was ever shoed can go down it."

" Indeed," laughed Dick.

A loud halloo from Major Mowbray, who seemed advancing upon the wings of the wind, told Dick that he was discovered. The major was a superb horseman, and took the lead of his party. Striking his spurs deeply into his horse, and giving him bridle enough, the major seemed to shoot forward like a shell through the air. The Burleigh Arms retired some hundred yards from the road, the space in front being occupied by a neat garden, with low clipped edges. No tall timber intervened between Dick and his pursuers, so that the motions of both parties were visible to each other. Dick saw in an instant, that, if he now started he should come into collision with the major exactly at the angle of the road, and he was by no means desirous of hazarding such a rencontre. He looked wistfully back at the double fence.

" Come into the stable—quick, captain, quick," exclaimed Ralph.

" The stable ?" echoed Dick, hesitatingly.

" Ay, the stable—it's your only chance. Don't you see he's turning the corner, and they are all coming—quick, sir, quick."

Dick lowered his head, rode into the tenement, the door of which was most unceremoniously slapped in the major's face, and bolted on the other side.

" Villain '" cried Major Mowbray, thundering at the door. " Come forth ! You are now fairly trapped at last—caught like the woodcock in your own spring. We have you—open the door, I say, and save us the trouble of forcing it. You cannot escape us. We will burn the building down, but we will have you."

"What do you want, measter?" cried Ralph from the lintel, whence he reconnoitred the major, and kept the door fast. "You're clean mistaken. There be no one here."

"We'll soon see that," said Paterson, who had now arrived, and leaping from his horse, the chief constable took a short run, to give himself impetus, and with his foot burst open the door. This being accomplished, in rushed the major and Paterson, but the stable was vacant. A door was open at the back. They rushed to it. The sharply sloping sides of a hill slipped abruptly downwards, within a yard of the door. It was a perilous descent to the horseman, yet the print of a horse's heels was visible in the dislodged turf and scattered soil.

"Confusion!" cried the major, "he has escaped us."

"He is yonder," said Paterson, pointing out Turpin moving swiftly through the steaming meadow. "See, he makes again for the road—he clears the fence. A regular throw he has given us, by the Lord!"

"Nobly done, by Heaven!" cried the major; "with all his faults I honour the fellow's courage, and admire his prowess. He's already ridden to-night as I believe never man rode before. I would not have ventured to slide down that wall, for it's nothing else, with the enemy at my heels. What say you, gentlemen, have you had enough. Shall we let him go, or——?"

"As far as chase goes, I don't care if we bring the matter to a conclusion," said Titus. "I don't think, as it is, that I shall have a *sate* to set on this week to come. I've lost leather most confoundedly."

"What says Mr. Coates?" asked Paterson. "I look to him."

"Then mount, and be off," cried Coates. Public duty requires that we should take him—and take him we will, or call me no lawyer."

"And *private pique*," returned the major. "No matter! the end is the same. Justice shall be satisfied. To your steeds, my merry men, all. Hark, and away!"

TURPIN'S HALT TO BAIT HIS MARE.

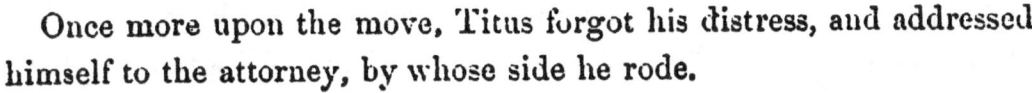

Once more upon the move, Titus forgot his distress, and addressed himself to the attorney, by whose side he rode.

"What place is that we are coming to?" asked he, pointing to a cluster of moonlit spires belonging to a town they were approaching.

"Stamford," replied Coates.

"Stamford!" exclaimed Titus; "By the powers! then we've ridden a matter of ninety miles. Why, the great deeds of Redmond O'Hanlon were nothing to this! I'll remember this to my dying day, and with reason," added he, uneasily shifting his position on the saddle.

CHAPTER IX.

EXCITEMENT.

DICK TURPIN, meanwhile, held bravely on his course, Bess was neither strained by the gliding passage down the slippery hill-side, nor shaken by *larking* the fence in the meadow. As Dick said, "it took a devilish deal to take it out of her." On regaining the high-road, she resumed her old pace, and once more they were distancing Time's swift chariot, in its whirling passage over the earth. Stamford, and the tongue of Lincoln's fenny shire, upon which it is situated, are past almost in a breath. Rutland is won, and passed, and Lincoln-shire once more entered. The road now verged within a bow-shot of that sporting Athens (Corinth, perhaps, we should say), Melton Mowbray. Melton then was unknown to fame, but, as if inspired by that *furor venaticus*, which now inspires all who come within twenty miles of this Charybdis of the chase, Bess here let out in a style with which it would have puzzled the Leicestershire squire's best prad

to have kept pace.   The spirit she imbibed through the pores of her skin, and the juices of the meat she had champed, seemed to have communicated preternatural excitement to her.   Her pace was absolutely terrific.   Her eyeballs were dilated, and glowed like flaming carbuncles ; while her widely distended nostril seemed, in the cold moonshine, to snort forth smoke, as from a hidden fire.   Fain would Turpin have controlled her—but, without bringing into play all his tremendous nerve, no check could be given her headlong course, and for once, and the only time in her submissive career, Bess resolved to have her own way—and she had it.   Like a sensible fellow, Dick conceded the point.   There was something even of conjugal philosophy in his self communion upon the occasion.   " E'en let her have her own way and be hanged to her, for an obstinate self-willed jade as she is," said he, " now her back is up there will be no stopping her, I'm sure, she rattles away like a woman's tongue, and when that once begins, we all know what chance the curb has.   Best to let her have it out, or rather to lend her a lift. 'Twill be over the sooner. Tantivy ! I know which of us will tire first."   With this conclusion, Dick pressed the sides of his gallant Black Bess, and continued his headlong career.

We have before said, that the vehement excitement of continued swift riding, produces a paroxysm in the sensorium amounting to delirium.   Dick's blood was again on fire.   He was first giddy, as after a deep draught of kindling spirit—this passed off, but the spirit was still in his veins—the *estro* was working in his brain.   All his ardour, his eagerness, his fury returned.   He rode like one insane, and his courser partook of the frenzy.   She bounded—she leaped— she tore up the ground beneath her—while Dick gave vent to his exultation in one wild prolonged halloo.   More than half the race is run.   He has triumphed over every difficulty.   He will have no further occasion to halt.   Bess carries her forage along with her. The course is straight-forward—success seems certain—the gaol already reached—the path of glory won.   Another wild halloo, to which the echoing woods reply, and away !

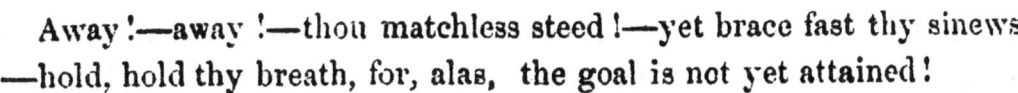

Away!—away!—thou matchless steed!—yet brace fast thy sinews
—hold, hold thy breath, for, alas, the goal is not yet attained!

> But forward! forward, on they go,
>   High snorts the straining steed,
> Thick pants the rider's labouring breath,
>   As headlong on they speed!

CHAPTER X,

THE GIBBET.

As the eddying current sweeps over its plains in howling bleak
December, the horse and her rider passed over what remained of Lin-
colnshire. Grantham is gone, and they are now more slowly looking
up the ascent of Gonerby-hill, a path well known to Turpin; where
often, in bye-gone nights, many a purse had changed its owner.
With that feeling of independence and exhilaration which every one
feels, we believe, on having climbed the hill side, Turpin turned to
gaze around him. There was triumph in his eye. But the triumph
was checked as his glance fell upon a gibbet near him to the right, on
the round point of hill, which is a landmark to the wide vale of Bel-
voir. Pressed as he was for time, Dick immediately struck out in the
road, and approached the spot where it stood. Two scarecrow objects
covered with rags and rusty links of chains, depended from the tree.
A night crow screaming round the carcasses, added to the hideous
effect of the scene. Nothing but the living highwayman and his ske-
leton brethren were visible upon the solitary spot. Around him was
the lonesome waste of hill, o'erlooking the moonlit valley—beneath

his feet a patch of bare and lightning-blasted sod—above, the wan, declining moon and skies, flaked with ghostly clouds—before him, the bleached bodies of the murderers, for such they were.

"Will this be my lot, I marvel?" said Dick, looking upwards, with an involuntary shudder.

"Ay, marry, will it," rejoined a crouching figure, suddenly springing from behind a tuft of briars that skirted the blasted ground.

Dick started in his saddle, while Bess reared and plunged, at the sight of this unexpected apparition.

"What, ho! thou devil's dam, Barbara, is it thou?" exclaimed Dick, re-assured, upon discovering that it was the gipsey queen, and no spectre, whom he beheld. "Stand still, Bess—stand, lass. What dost thou here mother of darkness? Art gathering mandrakes for thy poisonous messes, or pilfering flesh from the dead? Meddle not with their bones, or I will drive thee hence. What dost thou here, I say old dam of the gibbet?"

"I came to die here!" replied Barbara, in a feeble tone, and throwing back her hood, she displayed features well nigh as ghastly as those of the skeletons above her."

"Indeed," replied Dick. "You've made choice of a pleasant spot it must be owned. But you'll not die yet."

"Do you know whose bodies these are?" asked Barbara, pointing upwards.

"Two of your race," replied Dick; "right brethren of the blade."

"Two of my sons," returned Barbara; "my twin children. I am come to lay my bones beneath their bones—my sepulchre shall be their sepulchre; my body shall feed the fowls of the air as theirs have fed them. And if ghosts can walk, we'll scour this heath together. I tell you what Dick Turpin, said the hag, drawing as near to the highwayman, as Bess would permit her; "dead men walk and ride— aye, *ride* !—there's a comfort for you. I've seen these do it. I've seen them fling off their chains, and dance—aye, dance with me—with their mother. No revels like dead men's revels, Dick. I shall soon join 'em."

"You will not lay violent hands upon yourself, mother?" said Dick, with difficulty mastering his terror.

"No," replied Barbara, in an altered tone, "But I will let nature do her task. Would she could do it more quickly! Such a life as mine won't go out without a long struggle. What have I to live for now? All are gone. But what is this to you? You have no child—and if you had, you could not feel like a father—no matter!—I rave. Listen to me. I have crawled hither to die, 'Tis five days since I beheld you, and during that time, food has not passed these lips—nor aught of moisture, save heaven's dew, cooled this parched throat, nor shall they to the last. That time cannot be far off—and now, can you not guess *how* I mean to die?—Begone, and leave me —your presence troubles me. I would breathe my last alone, with none to witness the parting pang."

"I will not trouble you longer," mother," said Dick, turning his mare, "nor will I ask your blessing."

"Hence!" cried the crone—and as she watched Dick's figure lessening upon the waste, and at length beheld him finally disappear down the hill-side, she sank to the ground, her frail strength being entirely exhausted. "Body and soul may now part in peace," gasped she—"All I lived for is accomplished." And ere one hour had elapsed, the night crow was perched upon her still breathing frame.

CHAPTER XI.

THE PHANTOM STEED.

TIME presses. We may not linger on our course. We must fly on before our flying highwayman. Full forty miles shall we pass over

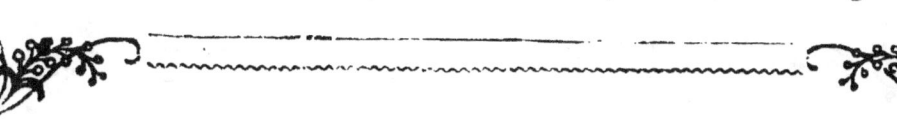

in a breath.   Two more hours have elapsed, and he still urges his headlong career, with heart resolute as ever, and purpose yet unchanged.   Fair Newark, and the dashing Trent, "most loved of England's streams," are gathered to his laurels.   Broad Notts and its heavy paths, and sweeping glade, its waste (forest no more), of Sherwood past; bold Robin Hood and his merry men, his Marian, and his moonlight rides recalled, forgotten, left behind—Hurrah! hurrah! that wild halloo—that waving arm—that enlivening shout.   What means it? He is once more upon Yorkshire ground; his horse's hoofs beat, once more, the soil of that noble shire.   So transported was Dick, that he could almost have flung himself from the saddle to kiss the dust beneath his feet, thrice fifty miles has he run, nor has the morn yet dawned upon his labours.   Hurrah! the end draws nigh. The gaol is in view—halloo—halloo—on!

Bawtrey is past.   He takes the lower road by Thorne and Selby. He is skirting the waters of the deep channelled Don.

Bess now began to manifest some slight symptoms of distress. There was a strain in the carriage of her throat—a dulness in her eye a laxity in her ear—and a slight stagger in her gait, which Turpin noticed with apprehension. Still she went on, though not at the same gallant pace as heretofore.   But, as the tired bird still battles with the blast upon the ocean—as the swimmer still stems the stream, though spent—on went she—nor did Turpin dare to check her, fearing, that if she stopped, she might loose her force, or if she fell, she would rise no more."

The moon had set, the stars

Pinnacled deep in the intense inane.

had all—save one, the herald of the dawn, withdrawn their lustre. A dull mist lay on the stream, and the air became piercing cold.   Turpin's chilled fingers could scarcely grasp the slackening rein, while his eyes, irritated by the keen atmosphere, hardly enabled him to distinguish surrounding objects, or even to guide his steed.   It was

owing, probably, to this latter circumstance, that Bess suddenly
floundered and fell, throwing her master over her head.

Turpin instantly recovered himself. His first thought was for his
horse. But Bess was instantly upon her legs—covered with dust and
foam, sides and cheeks—and with her large eyes glaring wildly,
almost piteously, upon her master.

"Art hurt, lass?" asked Dick, as she shook herself, and slightly
shivered. And he proceeded to the horseman's scrutiny. "Nothing
but a shake, though that dull eye, those quivering flanks," added he,
looking earnestly at her, "she won't go much further, and I must
give it up—what! give up the race just when it's won? No, that can't

No. 8

be. Ha! well thought on. I've a bottle of liquid, given me by an old fellow, who was a knowing cove, and famous jockey in his day, which he swore would make a horse go as long as he had a leg to carry him, and bade me keep it for some great occasion. I've never used it. But I'll try it now. It should be in this pocket. Ah! Bess, wench, I fear I'm using thee, after all, as Sir Luke did his mistress, that I thought so like thee. No matter! It will be a glorious end."

Raising her head upon his shoulder, Dick poured the contents of the bottle down the throat of his mare.—Nor had he to wait long, its invigorating effects were instantaneous. The fire was kindled in the glassy orb; her crest was once more erected; her flank ceased to quiver; and she neighed loud and joyously.

"Egad, the old fellow was right, cried Dick. "The drink has worked wonders. What the devil could it have been? It smells like spirit," added he, examining the bottle. "I wish I'd left a taste for myself. But here's that will do as well." And he drained the flask of the last drop of brandy.

Dick's limbs had now become so excessively stiff, that it was with difficulty he could remount his horse. But this necessary preliminary being achieved by the help of a stile, he found no difficulty in resuming his accustomed position upon the saddle. We know not whether there was any likeness between our Turpin and that modern Hercules of the sporting world, Mr. Osbaldeston. Far be it from us to institute any comparison, though we cannot help thinking that, in one particular, he resembled that famous "copper-bottomed squire."

Once more, at a gallant pace, he traversed the banks of the Don, skirting the fields of flax that bound its sides, and hurried far more swiftly than its current to its confluence with the Aire.

While involved in a fog, Turpin became aware of another horseman by his side. It was impossible to discern the features of the rider, but his figure in the mist seemed gigantic—neither was the colour of his steed distinguishable. Nothing was visible, except the meagre-looking, phantom-like outline of a horse and his rider, and,

as the unknown rode upon the turf that edged the way, even the sound of his horse's hoofs were scarcely audible. Turpin gazed, not without superstitious awe. Once or twice he essayed to address the strange horseman, but his tongue clove to the roof of his mouth. He fancied he discovered in the mist-exaggerated lineaments of the stranger a wild and fantastic resemblance to his friend, Tom King. "It must be Tom," thought Turpin ; "he's come to warn me of my approaching end. I will speak to him."

But terror o'ermastered his speech. He could not force out a word, and thus, side by side, they rode in silence. Quaking with fears he would scarcely acknowledge to himself, Dick watched every motion of his companion. He was still, stern, spectre-like, erect, and looked for all the world like a demon on his phantom steed. His courser seemed, in the indistinct outline, to be huge and bony, and as he snorted furiously in the fog, Dick's heated imagination supplied his breath with a due proportion of flame. Not a word was spoken—not a sound heard, save the sullen dead beat of his hoofs upon the grass. It was intolerable to ride thus cheek by jowl with a goblin. Dick could stand it no longer. He put spurs to his horse, and endeavoured to escape. But it might not be. The stranger, apparently without effort, was still by his side, and Bess's feet, in her master's apprehensions, were nailed to the ground. Bye and bye, however, the atmosphere became clearer. Bright quivering beams burst through the vaporous shroud, and then it was that Dick discovered that the apparition of Tom King was no other than Luke Rookwood. He was mounted on his old horse, Rook, and looked grim and haggard as a ghost vanishing at the crowing of the cock.

"Luke Rookwood by this light!" exclaimed Dick, in astonishment. "Why, I took you for——"

"The devil, no doubt!" returned Luke, smiling sternly, " and were sorry to find yourself so hard pressed. Don't disquiet yourself, I am still flesh and blood.

"Had I taken you for one of mortal mould," said Dick, " you should have soon seen where I'd have put you in the race. That

confounded fog deceived me, and Bess acted the fool as well as myself.
However, now I know you, Luke, you must spur alongside, for the
hawks are on the wing, and though I've much to say, I've not a
second to lose."   And Dick briefly detailed the particulars of his
ride.   "But in case of a break down on my part, suppose you take
charge of my purse, in the mean time."

Luke would have declined this offer.

"Pshaw!" said Dick.   "Who knows what may happen? and it's
not ill-lined either.   You'll find an odd hundred or so, in that silken
bag—it's not often a highwayman gives away a purse. Take it, man,
—we'll settle all to-night; and if I don't come, keep it, it will help
you to your bride.   And now off with you to the hut, for you are
only hindering me.   Adieu.   We'll do the trick to-night.   Away
with you to the hut.   Keep yourself snug there till midnight."

"At midnight," replied Luke, wheeling off, "I shall expect
you.

"Ware hawks!" halloed Dick.

But Luke had vanished.   In another instant Dick was scouring
the plain as rapidly as ever.   In the meantime, as Dick has casually
alluded to hawks, it may not be amiss to inquire how they had flown
throughout the night, and whether they were still in chase of their
quarry.

With the exception of Titus, who was completely done up at
Grantham;   "having got," as he said, "a complete belly-full of it,"
they were still on the wing, and resolved sooner or later to pounce
upon their prey—pursuing the same system as heretofore, in regard
to post-horses.   Major Mowbray and Paterson took the lead, but the
irascible and invincible attorney was not far in their rear, his wrath
having been by no means allayed by the fatigue he had undergone.
At Bawtry they held a council of war for a few minutes, being doubt-
ful which course he had taken.   Their incertitude was relieved by a
foot traveller who had heard Dick's loud halloo on passing the
boundary of Nottinghamshire, and had seen him take the lower road.
They struck, therefore, into the path to Thorne, at a hazard, and

were soon satisfied they were right. Furiously did they spur on. They reached Selby: changed horses at the inn in front of the venerable cathedral church, and learnt from the post-boy that a toil-worn horseman, on a jaded steed, had ridden through the town, about five minutes before them, and could not be more than a quarter of a mile in advance, "his horse was so dead beat," said the lad, "that I'm sure he cannot have got far, and if you look sharp, I'll be bound you'll overtake him before he reaches Cawood Ferry."

Mr. Coates was transported. "We'll lodge him snug in York Castle before an hour, Paterson," cried he, rubbing his hands.

"I hope so, Sir," said the constable, "but I begin to have some qualms."

"Now, Gentleman," shouted the post-boy, "come along, I'll soon bring you to him."

CHAPTER XII.

CAWOOD FERRY.

THE sun had just o'ertopped the "high eastern hill," as Turpin reached the Ferry of Cawood, and his beams were reflected upon the deep, and sluggish waters of the Ouse. Wearily had he dragged his course thither—wearily and slow. The powers of his gallant steed were spent, and he could scarcely keep her from sinking. It was now midway between the hours of five and six. Nine miles only lay before him—and that thought again revived him. He reached the water's edge, and hailed the ferry-boat, which was then on the other side of the river. At that instant a loud shout smote upon his ear—it was the halloo of his pursuers. Despair was in his look. He shouted to the

boatman, and bade him pull fast. The man obeyed—but he had
to breast a strong stream, and had a lazy bark and heavy skulls to
contend with. He had scarcely left the shore, when another shout
was raised from the pursuers. The tramp of their steeds grew louder
and louder.

The boat had scarcely reached the middle of the stream. His
captors were at hand. Quietly did he walk down the bank, and as
cautiously enter the water. There was a plunge, and steed and rider
were swimming down the river.

Major Mowbray was at the brink of the stream. He hesitated an
instant, and stemmed the tide. Seized, as it were, by a mania for
equestrian distinction, Mr. Coates braved the torrent. Not so with
Paterson. He very coolly took out his bull-dogs, and watching Turpin, cast up in his own mind the pros and cons of shooting him as he
was crossing. "I could certainly hit him," thought, or said, the constable, "but what of that? A dead highwayman is worth nothing—
alive he *weighs* 300*l*. I won't shoot him, but I'll make a pretence."
And he fired accordingly.

The shot skimmed over the water, but did not, as it was intended,
do much mischief. It, however, occasioned a mishap, which had
nearly proved fatal to our aquatic attorney. Alarmed at the report
of the pistol, in the nervous agitation of the moment, Coates drew in
his rein so tightly, that his steed instantly sank. A moment or two
afterwards he rose, shaking his ears, and floundering heavily towards
the shore; and such was the chilling effect of this sudden immersion,
that Mr. Coates now thought much more of saving himself, than of
capturing Turpin. Dick, meanwhile, had reached the opposite bank,
and, refreshed by her bath, Bess scrambled up the sides of the stream,
and speedily regained the road. " I shall do it, yet," shouted Dick ;
" that stream has saved her. Hark away, lass ! Hark away !"

Bess heard the cheering cry, and she answered to the call. She
roused all her energies—strained every sinew—and put forth all her
remaining strength. Once more, on wings of swiftness, she bore him
away from his pursuers, and Major Mowbray, who had now gained

the shore, and made certain of securing him, beheld him spring, like a wounded hare, from beneath his very hand. "It cannot hold out," said the major, "It is but an expiring flash, that gallant steed must soon drop."

"She be regularly booked, that's certain," said the post-boy. "We shall find her on the road."

Contrary to all expectations, however, Bess held on, and set pursuit at defiance. Her pace was swift as when she started. But it was unconscious and mechanical action. It wanted the ease, the lightness, the life of her former riding. She seemed screwed up to a task which she must execute, There was no flogging—no gory heel; but the heart was throbbing—tugging at the sides within. Her spirit spurred her onwards. Her eye was glazing—her chest heaving—her flank quivering—her crest again fallen. Yet she held on. "She is dying, by God!" said Dick. "I feel it." No, she held on.

Fulford is past. The towers and pinnacles of York burst upon him in all the freshness, the beauty, and the glory of a bright, clear, autumnal morn. The ancient city seemed to smile a welcome—a greeting. The noble minster, and its serene and massive pinnacles, crocketed, lantern-like, and beautiful; Saint Mary's lofty spire, All-Hallows tower, the massive mouldering walls of the adjacent postern, the grim castle, and Clifford's neighbouring keep—all beemed upon him, "like a bright-eyed face, that laughs out openly." "It is done —it is won!" cried Dick. "Hurrah, hurrah!" And the sunny air was cleft with his shouts.

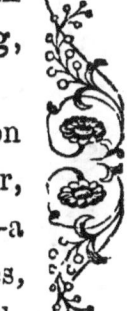

Bess was not insensible to her master's exultation. She neighed feebly in answer to his call, and reeled forwards. It was a piteous sight to see her—to mark her staring, protruding eye-ball—her skaking flanks—but while life and limb held together, she held on.

Another mile is past. York is near.

"Hurrah!" shouted Dick, but his voice was hushed. Bess tottered —fell. There was a dreadful gasp—a parting moan—a snort—her eye gazed for an instant upon her master, with a dying glare—then grew glassy, rayless, fixed. A shiver ran through her frame. Her heart had burst.

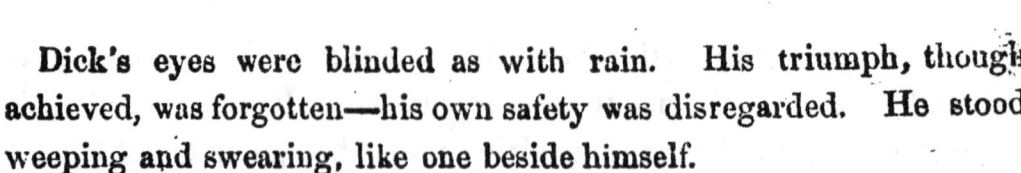

Dick's eyes were blinded as with rain. His triumph, though achieved, was forgotten—his own safety was disregarded. He stood weeping and swearing, like one beside himself.

"And art thou gone, Bess?" cried he, in a voice of agony, lifting up his courser's head, and kissing her lips, covered with blood-flecked foam. "Gone! gone! and I have killed the best steed that was ever crossed! And for what—for what?"

At that moment the deep bell of the minster clock tolled out the hour of six.

"I am answered," gasped Dick, "*it was to hear those strokes!*"

Turpin was roused from the state of stupefaction into which he had fallen by a smart slap on the shoulder. Recalled to himself by the blow, he started at once to his feet, while his hands sought his pistols —but he was spared the necessity of using them, by discovering in the intruder, the bearded visage of a gipsey, named Balthazar. He was habited in mendicant weeds, and sustained a large wallet upon his shoulders.

"So its all over with the best mare in England, I see," said Balthazar; "I can guess how it has happened—you are pursued."

"I am," said Dick, roughly.

"Your pursuers are at hand?"

"Within a few hundred yards."

"Then why stay here? Fly while you can."

"Never—never," cried Turpin; "I'll fight it out here—by Bess's side. Poor lass! I've killed her—but she has done it—ha, ha!— we have won—what?" and his utterance was again choked.

"Hark! I hear the tramp of horses, and shouts," cried the gipsey. "Take this wallet. You'll find a change of dress within it. Dart into that thick copse—save yourself."

"And Bess—I cannot leave her," exclaimed Dick, with an agonising look at his horse.

"And what did Bess die for, but for to save you?" rejoined the gipsey.

"True, true," said Dick; but take care of her. Don't let those dogs of hell meddle with her carcase."

THE DEATH

"Away," cried the gipsey, "leave Bess to me."

Possessing himself of the wallet, Dick disappeared in the adjoining copse.

He had not been gone many seconds when Major Mowbray rode up.

"Who is he?" exclaimed the major, flinging himself from his horse, and seizing the gipsey. "This is not Turpin."

"Certainly not," said Balthazar coolly. "I am not exactly the figure for a highwayman."

"Where is he? what has became of him?" asked Coates in despair, as he and Paterson joined the major.

"Escaped, I fear," replied the major. "Have you seen any one fellow?" added he, addressing the gipsey.

"I have seen no one," replied Balthazar. "I am only this instant arrived. This dead horse lying in the road attracted my attention.

"Ha!" exclaimed Paterson, leaping from his steed! "this may be Turpin after all. He has as many disguises as the devil himself, and may have carried that goat's hair in his pocket." Saying which, he seized the gipsey by the beard, and shook it with as little reverence as the Gaul handled the hirsute chin of the Roman senator.

"The devil! hands off," roared Balthazar. "By Salmon, I won't stand such usage. Do you think a beard liké mine is the growth of a few minutes? Hands off, I say,"

"Regularly done!" said Paterson, removing his hold of the gipsey's chin, and looking as blank as a cartridge.

"Ay," exclaimed Coates, "all owing to this worthless piece of carrion. If it were not that I hope to see him dangling from those walls," pointing towards the Castle, "I should wish her master were by her side now. To the dogs with her;" and he was about to spurn the breathless carcase of poor Bess, when a sudden blow, dealt by the gipsey's staff, felled him to the ground.

"I'll teach you to molest me," said Balthazar, about to attack Paterson.

"Come, come," said the discomfited chief constable, "no more

of this. It's plain we're in the wrong box. Every bone in my body aches sufficiently without the aid of your cudgel, old fellow. Come Mr. Coates take my arm, and let's be moving. We've had an infernal long ride for nothing."

" Not so," replied Coates; " I've paid pretty dearly for it. However, let us see if we can get any breakfast at the Bowling-green yonder ; though I've already had my morning draught," added the facetious man of law, looking at his dripping apparel.

" Poor Black Bess !" said Major Mowbray, wistfully regarding the body of the mare, as it lay stretched at his feet. " Thou deserved'st a better fate, and a better master. His exploits will, henceforth, want the colouring of romance, which thy unfailing energies threw over them. Light, lie the ground over thee, thou matchless mare !"

To the Bowling-green the party proceeded, leaving the gipsey in undisturbed possession of the lifeless body of Black Bess. Major Mowbray ordered a substantial repast to be prepared with all possible expedition

A countryman in a smock-frock was busily engaged at his morning's meal.

" To see that fellow bolt down his breakfast, one would think he had fasted for a month." said Coates; " see the wholesome effects of an honest industrious life, Paterson. I envy him his appetite —I should fall to with more zest, where Dick Turpin in his place."

The countryman looked up. He was an odd-looking fellow, with a terrible squint, and a strange contorted countenance.

" An ugly dog !" exclaimed Paterson ; " what a devil of a twist he has got !"

" What's that you says about Dick Taarpin, measter ?" asked the countryman, with his mouth half-full of bread.

" Have you seen aught of him ?" asked Coates.

" Not I," mumbled the rustic ; " but I hears aw the folk hereabouts talk of him. They say as how he sets all the lawyers and constables at defiance, and laughs in his sleeve at their efforts to catch him— ha—ha! He gets over more ground in a day, then they do in a week—ho—ho !"

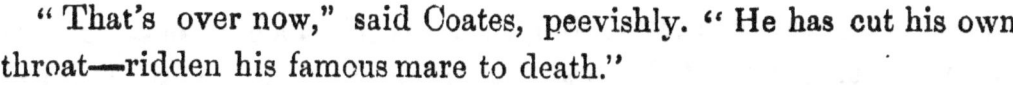

"That's over now," said Coates, peevishly. "He has cut his own throat—ridden his famous mare to death."

The countryman almost choked himself, in the attempt to bolt a huge mouthful. "Ay—indeed! measter. How happened that?" asked he, as soon as he recovered speech.

"The fool rode her from London to York, last night, returned Coates; "such a feat was never performed before. What horse could be expected to live through such work as that?"

"Ah, he were a foo' to attempt that," observed the countryman, "but you followed belike?"

"We did."

"And took him arter all, I reckon?" asked the rustic, squinting more horribly than ever.

"No," returned Coates, "I can't say we did—but we'll have him yet. I'm pretty sure he can't be far off. We may be nearer him than we imagine."

"May be so, measter," returned the countryman; "but might I be so bold as to ax how many horses you used in the chase—some half dozen, may be?"

"Half a dozen! "growled Paterson; "we had twenty at the least."

"And I ONE!" mentally ejaculated Turpin, for he was the countryman.

Dick Turpin, who thus accomplished the most extraordinary feat of horsemanship that was ever recorded, either in this or any other country, was hanged at York in 1739. His firmness deserted him not at the last. When he mounted the fatal tree his left leg trembled; he stamped it impatiently down, and, after a brief chat with the hangman, threw himself suddenly and resolutely from the ladder. The remains of the highwayman found a final resting-place in the desecrated churchyard of Saint George, without the Fishergate postern, a green and grassy cemetery, but withal a melancholy one. A few recent tombs mark out the spots where some of the victims of the pestilence of 1832-33 have been interred; and amongst them is a plain stone slab, bearing the simple initials,

R.T.

Beneath it rests the mortal remains of this once celebrated highwayman.

The irons by which he was fettered are still shown at York Castle, and are of prodigious weight and strength; and though the Herculean robber is said to have moved in them with ease, the present turnkey was scarcely able to lift the ponderous fetters. An old woman of the same city has a lock of hair, said to have been Turpin's, which she avouches her grandfather cut off from the body after the execution, and which the believers look upon with great reverence.

THE END.